# Henry Helps

## Wash the Car

written by **Beth Bracken**      illustrated by **Ailie Busby**

Raintree is an imprint of Capstone Global Library Limited, a company incorporated in England and Wales having its registered office at 264 Banbury Road, Oxford, OX2 7DY – Registered company number: 6695582

www.raintree.co.uk
myorders@raintree.co.uk

ISBN 978-1-4747-3132-4
21 20 19 18 17
10 9 8 7 6 5 4 3 2 1

British Library Cataloguing in Publication Data
A full catalogue record for this book is available from the British Library.

For Sam, the best helper I know. — BB

Henry loves cars.

He loves playing with his little cars,
and he loves riding in Mum's big car.

He even loves washing the car!

The first thing Henry does is put on his swimming trunks.

Then he gets a bucket, a sponge and a dry cloth.

Henry drags the hose across the garden.

It is really hard to pull!

Mum fills a bucket with soapy water.

Bubbles tickle Henry's toes.

Henry and Mum scrub the car.

They start at the top and work down.

They even scrub the tyres.

Then they use the hose to rinse it off.
The water gets all over Henry, too.

Henry helps Mum polish the car until it shines.

They use a special cleaner for the windows.

Now the car is perfectly clean.

And so is Henry!